for noah

It's A MiTig!

BRIDGET GEORGE

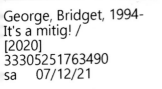

D&M
Kids

Giizis is rising, the day is brand new.
Let's learn some words nature's gathered for you.

From under the water

it jumps up for fun.

Covered in scales, it's an **ashigan.**

This creature has quills and nibbles a log.

Between leafy bushes, it's a ...

What wiggles and slithers and moves very quick?

Down on the ground, it's a

ginebig.

This animal whistles and lives in a tree.

Building a nest, it's a

bineshiinh.

Some critters throw acorns—

watch out below!

Climbing a tree, it's an **ajidamoo!**

Here we grow plants that soak up the sun.

At the edge of the trees, it's a **gitigaan.**

This bark-covered giant grows tall and thick,

covered in branches, it's a **mitig!**

What animal's toothy and plays with a stick?

It swims in the river, it's called an

amik.

Cold rushing water flows fast and free.

At the edge of the grass, it's a **ziibi.**

A small insect buzzes and bumbles on through.

It rests on a flower, it's an

a a m o o.

Growing where twigs end and fresh leaves begin,

little and round, it's a **mitigomin.**

Dibiki-giizis is glowing and bright.
You've learned many new words, now it's time for goodnight.

Pronunciation Guide

Learning a new language can be tricky. Let's learn how to say the Ojibwe words in this book by using sounds you might already know. Sometimes the ways people pronounce Ojibwe words sound different, depending on where they live and what they were taught. It's also important to note that Ojibwe words don't use stresses. Use this guide to help you while you learn.

OJIBWE VOWEL	SOUNDS LIKE	LOOKS LIKE
a	**a**bout	**a**jidamoo
aa	f**a**ther	g**aa**g
i	w**i**n or **i**t*	am**i**k
ii	fr**ee**	binesh**ii**nh
o	**o**kay	mitig**o**min
oo	fl**oa**t or sh**oo**t*	aam**oo**
e	d**ay**	gin**e**big

*depending on where you live

If you'd like to hear *It's a Mitig!* read aloud you can find recordings on the author's website, bridgetgeorge.com

GIIZIS

MITIG

ASHIGAN

BINESHIINH*

GINEBIG

AMIK

ZIIBI

MITIGOMIN

AJIDAMOO

GITIGAAN

GAAG

AAMOO

DIBIKI — GIIZIS

*Any time you see Ojibwe vowels followed by "nh", this combination of letters makes a special sound that you won't find in English. To hear this special sound, find the vowel on the chart on the previous page and plug your nose while you say it! After you hear the sound, try to make it without plugging your nose.

Douglas and McIntyre (2013) Ltd.
P.O. Box 219, Madeira Park, BC, V0N 2H0
www.douglas-mcintyre.com

Edited by Brianna Cerkiewicz and Sarah Harvey
With thanks to Margaret Ann Noodin
Printed and bound in South Korea

Douglas and McIntyre acknowledges the support of the Canada Council for the Arts, the Government of Canada, and the Province of British Columbia through the BC Arts Council.

Library and Archives Canada Cataloguing in Publication

Title: It's a mitig! / Bridget George.
Names: George, Bridget, 1994- author, illustrator.
Identifiers: Canadiana (print) 20200237209 | Canadiana (ebook) 20200237586 | ISBN 9781771622738 (hardcover) | ISBN 9781771622745 (EPUB)
Subjects: LCSH: Ojibwa language—Vocabulary—Juvenile literature. | LCSH: Nature—Juvenile literature. | LCGFT: Picture books.Classification: LCC PM851 .G46 2020 | DDC j497/.33381—dc23